This

Ladybird First Favourite Tale

belongs to

....

Published by Ladybird Books Ltd
A Penguin Company
Penguin Books Ltd, 80 Strand, London WC2R 0RL, UK
Penguin Books Australia Ltd, 707 Collins Street, Melbourne, Victoria 3008, Australia
Penguin Group (NZ) 67 Apollo Drive, Rosedale, North Shore 0632, New Zealand

003

© Ladybird Books Ltd MMXIV

ISBN: 978-0-72327-068-3

Printed in China

Ladybird First Favourite Tales

Puss in Boots

BASED ON A TRADITIONAL FOLK TALE
retold by Mandy Ross ★ illustrated by Ailie Busby

One sad day, a poor miller died. All he left to his youngest son was the mill's cat.

"A cat! What use is that?" sobbed the poor youngest son.

But *Miaow!* It was no ordinary cat.

"My master, I can help you," said the cat.
"But first I need a new pair of boots."

"Fancy that! A talking cat!" said the young man.
And with his last pennies, he bought a pair of
fine new boots.

Puss in Boots set to work. He put some grains of corn deep inside a good strong sack. Then off he went to the woods, and waited... a little way back.

Before long, some greedy partridges climbed into the sack. And...

Puss in Boots went to the palace to see the king.

"Your majesty, these partridges are for you,"
he said. "A gift from my master the count."

"Fancy that! A talking cat!" said the king.
"Thank you." And he filled Puss in Boots'
sack with gold coins.

"My master, these are for you!"
said Puss in Boots.
The young man's eyes opened wide.
"Fancy that! My clever cat!" he said.

Next day, Puss went to the palace again. "Your majesty, these rabbits are for you," he mewed. "A gift from my master the count."

"Fancy that! It's the talking cat!" said the king.

One day, Puss in Boots heard the king
was coming along the road.

"My master, quick!" whispered Puss in Boots.
"Off with your clothes! Jump in the river!"
The young man was puzzled. But he
did as Puss had told him.

"Help, your majesty!" said Puss in Boots.
"My master went for a swim – and look!
Robbers have stolen his clothes."

"It's the talking cat! Fancy that," said the king.
And he sent a servant to bring some of his own
clothes for the young man.

"My master, *miaow*, take a bow!" said Puss in Boots.

The king went on his way, and Puss ran ahead of him.

Some farmers were cutting hay.

"Farmers," said Puss in Boots, "the king is coming this way. Here's what you must say: this meadow belongs to the count."

"Fancy that! A talking cat!" said the farmers.

Then Puss ran ahead again, to where some woodcutters were chopping wood.

"Woodcutters," said Puss in Boots, "the king is coming this way. Here's what you must say: this forest belongs to the count."

Then Puss ran ahead again, to an ogre's palace.

"You are big, Ogre," mewed Puss in Boots.
"But are you clever, too?"

"Yes!" roared the ogre, as he turned himself into a lion.

"You are fierce, Ogre," mewed Puss in Boots.
"But can you turn yourself into a tiny mouse?"
"Yes!" squeaked the ogre.

Miaow! A very tasty mouse!

Then Puss gobbled up the mouse!

Soon the king arrived at the ogre's palace.

"Who owns this fine palace?" asked the king.

"Your majesty," mewed Puss.
"This palace belongs
to the count."

"Then the rich count must marry my daughter!" said the king.

So the miller's son married the king's daughter and he was never poor again.

"My master, *miaow*. Life is good now!" said Puss in Boots.

And they all lived happily ever after.

Collect the other books in the series

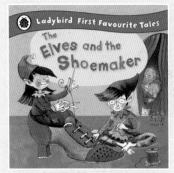

9781409306283

9781409309574

9781409306306

9781409309550

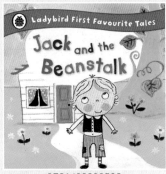

9781409309598

9781409309581

9781409306320

9781409306313

9781409306337